Copyright © 1988 by Nord-Süd Verlag AG, Gossau Zürich, Switzerland
First published in Switzerland under the title *Ein Esel geht nach Bethlehem*
English translation copyright © 1988 by North-South Books Inc.

First published in the United States, Great Britain, Canada,
Australia, and New Zealand in 1988 by North-South Books,
an imprint of Nord-Süd Verlag AG, Gossau Zürich, Switzerland.
First paperback edition published in 1998.

Distributed in the United States by North-South Books Inc., New York.

Library of Congress Catalog Card Number: 87:73271
Library of Congress Cataloging-in-Publication Data is available.
A CIP catalogue record for this book is available from The British Library.
ISBN 1-55858-952-X (paperback) 10 9 8 7 6 5 4 3 2 1
Printed in Belgium

For more information about our books, and the authors and artists
who create them, visit our web site: http://www.northsouth.com

The Little
Donkey

A Christmas story by Gerda Marie Scheidl

Retold and Illustrated by

Bernadette Watts

North-South Books
New York / London

Long ago, a baby was born in a stable in Bethlehem. His mother laid him to sleep in a manger full of hay, for there was no other place for him. Many people traveled from far and wide to see the baby for themselves because they believed he was born to be King.

News of the new King's birth even reached the ears of a little donkey. But the donkey's master told him the story was untrue and forbade him to go to Bethlehem, saying, "A king is born in a palace, not in a stable."

But the donkey believed the story, and he longed to visit the
new King. His longing filled his heart. He knew he must leave his
master and go to his King. So at nightfall, he quietly left.

At every step the little donkey had to fight his fear of the darkness. Yet as he trotted along he knew that every mile brought him closer to Bethlehem. He struggled through brambles and tripped over rocks and boulders. But, he thought only of the new King.

Soon he met a camel.

"Where are you going?" the camel inquired.

"To Bethlehem. I am going to visit the new King."

The camel sneered, "Nonsense! You would not be allowed to visit a king; you would be chased away!"

"Why?" asked the donkey sadly.

"Because you are a donkey; and a donkey is a lowly, stupid beast," answered the camel haughtily, as he strolled on.

The little donkey was hurt and confused. He nearly turned around to go home.

"No!" he said stubbornly to himself. "No, I will not give up my journey. I will go on, and I will visit the new King." He stamped his hooves, and then trotted onward along the stony pathway.

Suddenly a lion appeared out of the darkness. The donkey told the lion he was on his way to visit the new King. The lion roared with great disdain, "No king would want a visit from you. Look at me! King of all the animals. I am the only animal important enough to visit another king." He tossed his mane and turned his back on the humble donkey.

A hyena slunk up. "You silly donkey! Do you believe any king would even notice you? You were born to bear loads, not to stand in the presence of a king."

She laughed spitefully and disappeared into the night.

Many other animals passed by the donkey. A desert fox stared rudely; a wolf snarled and snapped at the little donkey's ankles. A ram pushed him aside roughly.

The little donkey felt so worthless that he dared not hold his head up. It was so dark he stumbled about and began to lose his way. Was there not even one star to comfort him?

Suddenly a great light seemed to surround the little donkey. His fear and distress faded into the darkness. Slowly, he lifted his head, and he saw above him angels in golden robes who guided him once again onto the road to Bethlehem.

Soon Bethlehem was only a few steps away. Right over a stable
close by the road stood a glorious star that flooded the world with
light. The donkey's heart overflowed with joy and wonder.
He came to the door of the stable and stepped in.

There in the hay, just as the story had said, lay the little child, and Mary and Joseph stood by him. The baby laughed merrily to see the donkey. He stretched out his hands to him and smiled. The little donkey bowed before his King. His journey had ended.